The Little
Star

First published in 2000
Franklin Watts
96 Leonard Street
London
EC2A 4XD

Franklin Watts Australia
45-51 Huntley Street
Alexandria
NSW 2015

A CIP catalogue record for this book is available
from the British Library.

ISBN 0 7496 3713 7 (hbk)
ISBN 0 7496 3833 8 (pbk)

Series Editor: Louise John
Series Advisor: Dr Barrie Wade
Series Designer: Jason Anscomb

Printed in China

The Little Star

by Deborah Nash

Illustrated by Richard Morgan

W
FRANKLIN WATTS
LONDON • SYDNEY

Little Star looked down
from the sky.

"I want to live down there,"
said Little Star.

6

"You can't," said his mum. "That's the Earth and you're a star."

Little Star was very sad.

He went to visit the Moon.

"It's fun living in the sky,"
said the Moon.

"Come with me, I can show you."

Little Star and the Moon
zoomed round the
Milky Way.

They bounced up and down
on soft, fluffy clouds.

They cooked sausages
by the heat of the Sun.

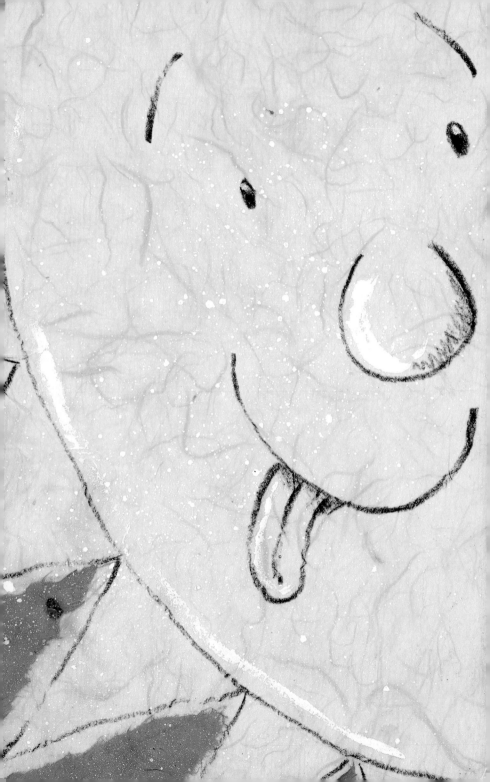

They slid down a rainbow.

18

They played football
with the planets.

"The sky is not so bad, after all," said Little Star.

"In fact, I think I like it!"

Little Star's mum and dad
were glad he wanted to sta

25

Little Star flew high up
into the sky.

Down on earth, people saw him shoot by.

"What's that up there?"
a little boy asked.

"It's a shooting star,"
said his dad.

"I want to live up there," said the little boy.

"You can't," said his dad.

"You're a boy, not a star!"

Leapfrog has been specially designed to fit the requirements of the National Literacy Strategy. It offers real books for beginning readers by top authors and illustrators.

There are 31 Leapfrog stories to choose from:

The Bossy Cockerel

Written by Margaret Nash, illustrated by Elisabeth Moseng

Bill's Baggy Trousers

Written by Susan Gates, illustrated by Anni Axworthy

Mr Spotty's Potty

Written by Hilary Robinson, illustrated by Peter Utton

Little Joe's Big Race

Written by Andy Blackford, illustrated by Tim Archbold

The Little Star

Written by Deborah Nash, illustrated by Richard Morgan

The Cheeky Monkey

Written by Anne Cassidy, illustrated by Lisa Smith

Selfish Sophie

Written by Damian Kelleher, illustrated by Georgie Birkett

Recycled!

Written by Jillian Powell, illustrated by Amanda Wood

Felix on the Move

Written by Maeve Friel, illustrated by Beccy Blake

Pippa and Poppa

Written by Anne Cassidy, illustrated by Philip Norman

Jack's Party

Written by Ann Bryant, illustrated by Claire Henley

The Best Snowman

Written by Margaret Nash, illustrated by Jörg Saupe

Eight Enormous Elephants

Written by Penny Dolan, illustrated by Leo Broadley

Mary and the Fairy

Written by Penny Dolan, illustrated by Deborah Allwright

The Crying Princess

Written by Anne Cassidy, illustrated by Colin Paine

Jasper and Jess

Written by Anne Cassidy, illustrated by François Hall

The Lazy Scarecrow

Written by Jillian Powell, illustrated by Jayne Coughlin

The Naughty Puppy

Written by Jillian Powell, illustrated by Summer Durantz

Freddie's Fears

Written by Hilary Robinson, illustrated by Ross Collins

Cinderella

Written by Barrie Wade, illustrated by Julie Monks

The Three Little Pigs

Written by Maggie Moore, illustrated by Rob Hefferan

Jack and the Beanstalk

Written by Maggie Moore, illustrated by Steve Cox

The Three Billy Goats Gruff

Written by Barrie Wade, illustrated by Nicola Evans

Goldilocks and the Three Bears

Written by Barrie Wade, illustrated by Kristina Stephenson

Little Red Riding Hood

Written by Maggie Moore, illustrated by Paula Knight

Rapunzel

Written by Hilary Robinson, illustrated by Martin Impey

Snow White

Written by Anne Cassidy, illustrated by Melanie Sharp

The Emperor's New Clothes

Written by Karen Wallace, illustrated by François Hall

The Pied Piper of Hamelin

Written by Anne Adeney, illustrated by Jan Lewis

Hansel and Gretel

Written by Penny Dolan, illustrated by Graham Philpot

The Sleeping Beauty

Written by Margaret Nash, illustrated by Barbara Vagnozzi